HAPPY LITTLE SQUIRREL

Ge Cuilin & Yi Ping
Illustrated by Tang Yunhui

NEW FRONTIER PUBLISHING

Little Squirrel was always happy.

For one spring and one summer,
he had lived in a beautiful wooden treehouse.

When autumn came, Little Squirrel began to collect
pine cones for winter.

One day, while he was away from his house, a heavy
rainstorm struck.

The wind and the rain battered his treehouse. It fell to the ground and broke into pieces.

Little Squirrel spent the night sheltering near a rock.

When Little Squirrel woke the next morning, he felt sad.

His treehouse was gone. Where would he live now?

As he stared up at the sky, he saw a tree with a hole in it.

'This will be the perfect house!' Little Squirrel thought.

He put some leaves on the floor and nailed a sign to the tree.

One day, Little Squirrel found a tiny bird whose nest
had fallen from a branch. Little Squirrel took her to his
new home and looked after her.

Then he met a rabbit with an injured paw. The rabbit
came to stay in Little Squirrel's home too.

Soon Little Squirrel's hole in the tree
was filled with animals who were hurt
or needed a place to live. It was a warm,
cosy shelter where the animals knew
they would be welcome.

Little Squirrel loved it when his new friends sang songs together and shared their stories.

His home became their home too.

As the weather began to turn cold, Little Squirrel
had a new visitor.

It was a fox.

He was not injured or lost, but Little Squirrel invited
him to come inside.

The fox didn't sing, and he didn't share his stories. He just ate and slept all day and night.

The next day, while Little Squirrel was out, the fox sent all the other animals away from Little Squirrel's home.

When Little Squirrel came back, the fox wouldn't let him inside. 'This is my home now,' the fox said.

Little Squirrel was homeless once again.

All his friends were angry, but Little Squirrel stayed calm. He was sure he could find them another home before winter came.

A friendly eagle heard about Little Squirrel's problem. She took Little Squirrel to see a cave in a mountainside.

'This is the best house ever!' cried Little Squirrel.

His friends brought him lots of gifts when he moved into his new home.

One frozen winter day, Little Squirrel
heard crying.

He looked outside his cave and saw the
fox, trembling with cold.

'My tree … it blew down in the wind. My hole is gone!' sobbed the fox. 'Can I please stay here with you?'

Before Little Squirrel could answer, the rabbit spoke up.

'Will you tell everyone that this is Little Squirrel's house and promise not to take it for yourself?' asked the rabbit sternly.

The fox wrote his promise on a leaf, but the leaf broke. He tried to write it on the snow and the ice, but it melted when he touched it.

So the fox told everyone it was Little Squirrel's house, and the rabbit recorded his words.

'Thank you,' said Little Squirrel kindly, and the fox blushed bright red.

Everyone was welcome in Little Squirrel's house.

First published in the UK in 2018
by New Frontier Publishing Europe Ltd
93 Harbord Street, London SW6 6PN
www.newfrontierpublishing.co.uk

ISBN: 978 1 912076 76 5 (HB)

A CIP catalogue record for this book is available from
the British Library.

Designed by Celeste Hulme

Printed in China
10 9 8 7 6 5 4 3 2 1